PUFFIN BOOKS

TOY STORY 2

Slinky, Mr Potato Head, Rex, Buzz and Hamm walked across the rooftop towards the edge. Mr Potato Head grabbed the end of Slinky's coil and jumped off the roof, using Slinky as a bungee rope. 'Geronimo!' he shouted as he landed safely on the lawn below.

Hamm jumped next, and then Rex. Buzz walked back to the window. 'We'll be back before Andy gets home,' he told the others.

The toys inside gathered at the window and waved goodbye. 'To Al's Toy Barn – and beyond!' Buzz shouted as he leapt off the roof. Slinky jumped last. The search for Woody had begun!

DISNEY · PIXAR

Adapted by Leslie Goldman

PUFFIN BOOKS

PUFFIN BOOKS

Published by the Penguin Group
Penguin Books Ltd, 27 Wrights Lane, London W8 5TZ, England
Penguin Putnam Inc., 375 Hudson Street, New York, New York 10014, USA
Penguin Books Australia Ltd, Ringwood, Victoria, Australia
Penguin Books Canada Ltd, 10 Alcorn Avenue, Toronto, Ontario, Canada M4V 3B2
Penguin Books (NZ) Ltd, Private Bag 102902, NSMC, Auckland, New Zealand

On the World Wide Web at: www.penguin.com

Penguin Books Ltd, Registered Offices: Harmondsworth, Middlesex, England

First published in the USA by Disney Press 1999
First published in Puffin Books 2000
1 3 5 7 9 10 8 6 4 2

Set in Clarendon Light

Made and printed in England by Clays Ltd, St Ives plc

British Library Cataloguing in Publication Data
A CIP catalogue record for this book is available from the British Library

ISBN 0-140-30745-5

Chapter One

Buzz Lightyear sped through the dark sky, the lights on his space suit flashing. He zeroed in on his target – a huge red planet. As the clouds surrounding the planet drifted away, he soared through, landing smoothly on the rocky surface. He raised his walkie-talkie to contact his headquarters. 'Buzz Lightyear mission log: all signs point to this planet as the location of Zurg's fortress.' Buzz glanced in all directions across the surface of the deserted planet. 'But there seems to be no sign of intelligent life anywhere.'

Just as he was starting to relax, Buzz spotted a group of red laser light beams. Seconds later, he found himself surrounded by armed robot forces. He raised his laser gun towards a crystal formation near by and fired. A huge explosion blew the robots away. But he hadn't destroyed the enemy completely. From the wall of the crater, a robotic camera moved swiftly towards Buzz. He took aim once more and fired.

He was able to destroy the camera, but then he felt something shifting under his feet. Before he could move, the ground gave way beneath him and he fell into a long, dark, deep cavern.

Landing on the ground, Buzz spotted a maze. There was no other way to go, so he entered it. He didn't realize that a blinking orange dot was on his back. The evil Zurg was monitoring Buzz's every step.

'Come to me, my prey,' Zurg growled from his control room.

Buzz walked through a door, and it closed behind him. Suddenly, deadly spikes shot out from the door and zoomed towards Buzz. He ran down the tunnel and jumped through another door with about a millisecond to spare. The spikes banged against the closed door, piercing its surface.

Buzz was safe for now. He made his way across a thin, swinging rope bridge, only to come face to face with Zurg.

'Buzz Lightyear! Your defeat will be my

greatest triumph!' shouted Zurg, as he took aim with his ion blaster.

'Not today, Zurg,' bellowed Buzz, as he raised his shield to deflect Zurg's bullet. Then he hurled the shield at Zurg, hitting him directly in the face.

Momentarily stunning Zurg, Buzz leapt over him and fired one shot. It curved to Zurg's left, narrowly missing.

Zurg recovered and took aim again, blasting Buzz and blowing his torso off. 'Ahh-ha-ha!' laughed a triumphant Zurg.

GAME OVER flashed in red across the screen.

CHAPTER TWO

Andy Davis was out of sight, so his toys were playing on their own. The real Buzz Lightyear and his friend and fellow toy Rex, a plastic dinosaur, jumped up to the TV screen.

'Ooooh, now that's gotta hurt,' Buzz said, in sympathy.

Rex stamped his feet. 'No! I'm never gonna defeat Zurg! I give up,' he shouted.

'Come on. Pull yourself together, Rex. Remember, a Space Ranger must turn and face his fears, no matter how ugly it gets. You must not flinch!'

'OK, one more round,' Rex pleaded.

He turned back to the TV screen.

'Ah!' shouted Rex. Woody's sudden appearance across the screen had startled him.

Ignoring Rex's whimpering, Woody

looked down at his Etch-A-Sketch slate and spoke to Buzz. 'OK, here's a list of things to do while I'm gone. Batteries need to be changed. Toys in the bottom of the chest need to be rotated. And make sure everyone attends Mr Spell's seminar on "what to do if you or a part of you is swallowed". OK?'

Buzz shook his head. 'Woody, you haven't found your hat yet, have you?'

'No,' said Woody. 'Andy's leaving for Cowboy Camp any minute now, and I can't find it anywhere!'

'Don't worry. In just a few hours you'll be sitting around a crackling campfire with Andy,' said Buzz. 'Has anyone found Woody's hat yet?' he called to the rest of the toys.

Green army men swarmed around the open toy box and some climbed down from the open lid into the box. 'Hut. Hut. Hut . . .' they chanted.

The Sergeant approached Buzz and saluted. 'Negatori. Still searching.'

Ham sat on the windowsill, looking outside through Lenny, the toy binoculars.

'The lawn gnome next door says it's not in the yard, but he'll keep looking,' Ham reported back.

Bo Peep and the Troll Doll walked into the

5

room. 'It's not in Molly's room. We've looked everywhere,' Bo Peep reported, shrugging.

Mr Potato Head peeped out from under the bed. 'I found it,' he shouted.

'You found my hat?' Woody said, cheering up.

'Your hat? Nah. The Mrs lost her earring again. Oh my little sweet potato!' He held up a plastic ear with a dangling earring attached.

Mrs Potato Head walked up with a huge grin painted across her face. 'You found it! It's so good to have a big strong spud around the house!' She took the ear and plugged it back into her ear socket.

Woody walked over to Andy's packed duffle bags and gave one of them a kick. 'Great. That's just great! This'll be the first year I miss Cowboy Camp, all because of my stupid hat.'

'Woody, look under your boot,' said Bo.

'Bo, don't be silly. My hat's not under my boot.'

'Just look,' she said.

Woody sighed and then raised his foot and looked at it. 'There, see? No hat. Just the word Andy.'

'Uh-hu,' said Bo, smiling. 'And the boy who wrote that would take you to camp with or without your hat.'

Woody stared at the signature and smiled. Bo was right. 'I'm sorry, Bo. It's just that I've been looking forward to this all year. It's my one time with just me and Andy.'

Bo grinned, and snared Woody with the crook of her stick. She pulled him towards her. 'You're cute when you care.'

'Everyone's looking,' whispered a blushing Woody.

'Let 'em look,' she said, and kissed him.

Someone turned the TV on and a clucking chicken blared out from the set. It was a commercial. A large man dressed in a chicken suit was flapping his wings on top of Al's Toy Barn.

'Hey, kids,' he clucked. 'This is Al, from Al's Toy Barn. And I'm sitting on some good deals here . . . Ow! Ah think I'm feelin' a deal hatchin' right now! Let's see what we got!' The man squinted and squirmed, then he stood up to reveal a giant egg. It cracked open and a giant $1 sign appeared on the screen. A bunch of toys floated across the screen. 'We got boats for a buck, beanies for a buck, boomerangs . . .'

'Turn it off,' shouted Woody. 'Someone's going to hear.'

The TV went on blaring, '. . . banjos for a buck, buck, buck!' Al flapped his chicken wings. 'And that's cheap, cheap, cheap!' A map flashed on the screen, and Al pointed to the Toy Barn.

Hamm, the piggy bank, waddled forward, grabbed the remote control, and turned off the TV. 'I despise that chicken,' he complained.

Slinky inched his wiry silver body into the room. 'OK,' he gasped, out of breath. 'I got good news and I got bad news.'

'What, what?' asked the toys.

'Good news is, I found Woody's hat!' Slinky wagged his tail – upon which was perched Woody's hat.

'My hat!' shouted Woody. 'Aw, Slink . . . thank you! Thank you!'

'What's the bad news?' asked Buzz.

'Here it comes!' Slinky shouted.

CHAPTER THREE

A snuffling sound pierced through the low chatter. It grew louder and then even louder, and then it turned into a bark.

'Aaah! It's Buster,' Rex shouted.

The toys rushed to the door in an attempt to prevent the inevitable. They all strained, but the pressure was too great. The dog's wet nose nudged through the crack in the door and the toys knew it wasn't stopping there.

'Woody! Hide! Quick!' Bo called out.

With a yelp, Woody dived into Andy's duffle bag and burrowed underneath some clothes and a baseball glove.

The door suddenly swung opened. Buster, a caramel-coloured dachshund, jumped triumphantly into the middle of the room. He barked loudly and ran around

9

the room, scattering toys and dribbling everywhere.

Etch spun away quickly in order to avoid Buster, but Buster, noticing the movement, pounced, flattening him. Buster panted, looked around and then continued his rampage.

As soon as Buster moved on, Etch wobbled to a standing position. The remains of his picture were covered with paw prints.

Suddenly Buster sniffed and turned towards the pile of bags. He ran over to the duffle bag, pulled Woody out, and flung him into the air. Woody landed in the middle of the room, lifeless.

Buster jumped on top of Woody, lips curled. He growled for a second, and then began to lick him.

'OK, OK,' Woody spluttered. 'You found me, Buster. All right. Hey, how'd he do, Hamm?'

Hamm stood in front of Mr Spell's read-out of 13.5. 'Eh, looks like a new record!'

Woody snapped his fingers. 'OK, boy. Sit. Stick em 'up! Pow!'

Feigning death, Buster yelped and fell over.

'Great job, boy,' said Woody, scratching

Buster's belly. 'Who's gonna miss me while I'm gone? Who's gonna miss me?'

Suddenly, voices from the hallway drifted into Andy's bedroom.

'Andy? You got all of your stuff?' It was Andy's mum, Mrs Davis.

'It's in my room,' said Andy.

Woody gasped and ran off to take up his position. All the other toys froze where they were and lay lifeless.

Andy kicked his bedroom door open with one cowboy boot. He walked in, revealing his full cowboy outfit. Buster barked and ran to Andy. 'Stick 'em up,' shouted Andy, pulling his toy guns out of the holster on his belt.

Buster left the room, and headed down the stairs.

'I guess we'll work on that later,' Andy said, putting down his toy guns. He walked up to Woody, who was propped up on his bag. 'Hey, Woody. Ready to go to cowboy camp?'

'Andy, honey,' his mother called. 'Five minutes and we're leaving.'

Andy began to play with Woody. He picked up Buzz too. They began to shake hands but, to Andy's shock and dismay, Woody's arm ripped!

'Andy, let's go,' Mrs Davis called up to him. She poked her head into Andy's room. 'What's wrong?' she asked.

'Woody's arm ripped!' gasped Andy.

'Maybe we can fix him on the way?' Mrs Davis suggested.

'No, let's just leave him,' Andy sighed, tossing Woody aside.

'I'm sorry, honey. But you know, toys don't last for ever.' Mrs Davis put Woody on the highest shelf in Andy's room, among a pile of old books. Then she and Andy left the room.

Seconds later, the toys came back to life. They stared up at Woody. 'What just happened?' they wanted to know.

'Woody's been shelved,' Mr Potato Head cried.

Woody scrambled to the edge of his shelf and looked out through the window. Andy and his mother were getting into their van. 'Andy!' he shouted.

But it was too late. The van pulled away.

CHAPTER FOUR

It was a long and hot summer on the shelf. The sun rose early one August morning. Woody was shaken from sleep by the sound of a van pulling up in front of the house. Once more, he looked out of the window.

Andy jumped out of the car, riding a Hobby Horse. 'Yee-haw! Ride 'em, cowboy! Whoa! Yeah! Giddyap! Giddyap!'

'He's back,' Woody whispered. He glanced down. Rex, Slinky, Mr Potato Head and Rocky were sitting, playing cards, at the foot of the bed. 'Hey, everybody! Andy's back! He's back early from Cowboy Camp!'

They heard Andy bound up the steps.

'Places, everyone! Andy's coming,' shouted Hamm.

The toys dropped their cards and

scattered. Woody froze in his 'toy pose' just as Andy burst into the room.

Andy ran up to Woody and pulled him down from the shelf. 'Hey, Woody! Did you miss me? Giddy-up, giddy-up. Ride 'em cowboy!' Andy walked Woody across the floor, swinging his arms. Suddenly Andy's smile faded. 'Oh, I forgot,' he said to Woody. 'You're broken.' He stared at Woody, frowning. 'I don't want to play with you any more.' And, with that, Andy let Woody drop.

Woody landed, forlorn, in a bin full of broken toy parts. He tried desperately to crawl out of the bin. 'Andy!' he shouted, struggling as toy arms pulled him back to the bottom of the bin.

Andy stared into the bin. 'Bye, Woody!' he said and closed the lid.

Next morning, Woody woke up, back on Andy's shelf. 'Huh? What's going on?' He glanced around the room, confused . . . until he realized that it had all been a bad dream. He got up, and his broken arm bumped into a pile of books, knocking them over. A pile of dust arose, and Woody coughed. Soon he noticed that he wasn't the only one coughing.

'What's going on? Wheezy, is that you?'

he said to a small stuffed penguin.

'Hey, Woody,' said Wheezy.

'What are you doing up here? I thought Mum took you to get your squeaker fixed months ago. Andy was so upset . . .' Woody said, confused.

'Nah,' Wheezy replied, motioning with one fuzzy wing. 'She just told Andy that to calm him down. Then, she shelved me.'

'Why didn't you yell for help?' Woody asked.

'I tried squeaking,' Wheezy said, shrugging. 'But I'm still broken. No one could hear me.' Wheezy squinted his eyes, and tried to squeak. The only sound that emerged was a pathetic, wavery little yelp. He coughed again and explained to Woody: 'The dust aggravates my condition. Cough, hack, wheeze!' Wheezy fell into Woody's arms, exhausted.

'What's the point of prolonging the inevitable?' Wheezy gasped. 'We're all just one stitch away from here . . . to there.' He pointed outside.

Woody looked out of the window and gasped. Mrs Davis was pounding a 'Yard Sale' sign into the ground.

CHAPTER FIVE

Woody called down to the other toys: 'Yard sale! Yard sale! Wake up, everyone! There's a yard sale outside!'

Buzz and Slinky stirred from their snooze. 'Huh?' Slinky asked, stretching his coiled body out.

'Yard sale?' Buzz repeated.

Sharky, Snake and Troll all popped their heads out of Andy's toy chest.

'Sarge! Emergency roll-call,' said Woody.

Sarge burst out over the top of the 'Bucket-O-Soldiers', saluting Woody. 'Sir! Yes, sir!'

He went around to gather all the toys together. 'Red alert!' he called through his mini-microphone. 'All civilians fall into position! NOW!'

The toys responded quickly and lined up.

'Single file! Let's move, move, move!'

Buzz marched over and began to write on the magic slate.

'Hamm?' he called.

'Here,' Hamm shouted.

'Potato Head, Mr and Mrs?'

'Here,' said Mrs Potato Head.

Buzz continued. 'Troikas, check.'

The Troikas opened up, smaller ones popping up out of the larger. 'Check, check, check, check.'

Buzz continued the roll-call. 'Slinky?'

'Yo.'

Rex quivered. 'Oh, I hate yard sales.'

Suddenly there was a bump from behind Andy's door. 'Ahh, someone's coming!' Rex warned everyone.

The toys resumed their old positions and froze. Woody hid Wheezy back behind the ABC book on the shelf and was returning to his old place just as the door began to creak open.

Mrs Davis entered with a box marked '25 cents'. She dug under Andy's bed and stuffed a pair of blue-and-silver velcro shoes in the box. She picked up Rex, who was trying to hide his look of utter panic. Luckily, she sat Rex on a table; she was moving him so she could get at the puzzle he was sitting on.

Next she reached up to the top shelf where Woody and Wheezy were, and took down the ABC Book. Woody sighed but, seconds later, Mrs Davis reached for Wheezy. 'HSSSS . . . HSSSS' Wheezy squeaked, as he was dropped into the box. 'Bye, Woody,' he whispered as he was carried out of the room.

Woody gasped. 'Not Wheezy. Oh, c'mon, think, Woody, think . . . think.' He had to do something.

Woody raised his good arm and let out a loud whistle. Buster came bounding into the room.

'Here, boy. Here, Buster, up here!' Woody called. He tried to climb down from the shelf, but he slipped because of his bad arm. He began to fall towards the hard wooden floor. Buster scrambled towards Woody and caught him at the last second.

'Ooof!' Woody groaned. He propped himself up on Buster's back and patted his matted fur. 'OK, boy, to the yard sale.'

'Did he say yard sale?' Mr Potato Head asked the others.

'He's crazy!' all the toys agreed.

CHAPTER SIX

Out on the front lawn, Woody and Buster hid behind an armchair at the edge of the yard sale. They peered around the chair, checking to see whether the coast was clear. 'OK, boy,' Woody whispered into Buster's ear. 'Let's go, boy. And keep it casual.'

They inched their way towards the table with the '25 cents' box. Buster paused at the edge of the table, and Woody jumped on to it. He hid for a moment behind a tall pepper grinder. Then he ran over to the box, hoisted himself up and jumped inside.

Seconds later, Woody was in the middle of rescuing Wheezy. He pushed Wheezy up and over the edge of the box, and then jumped out himself. They both ran over to Buster, and Woody tucked Wheezy into Buster's collar. 'There you go, pal.'

'Bless you, Woody,' Wheezy wheezed.

'All right now, back to Andy's room, where we belong,' Woody said, as he climbed on to Buster's back himself.

'Way to go, cowboy!' shouted the other toys, who were watching from the upstairs window.

They bounced back to victory, but Wheezy started to slip out from under Buster's collar. 'Woody . . . I'm slip'n . . . oh, oh,' he chanted with each bounce.

Woody held on to Wheezy with his good arm. But when Buster had to jump over a skateboard that lay in their path, Woody was thrown to the ground. The hound kept on running, oblivious, leaving Woody flat on his back in the grass.

Woody lifted his head, and watched Buster and Wheezy make their way back into the house. He groaned. But the worst was yet to come.

'Mummy, mummy! Look at this!' shouted a little girl. Her body cast a large shadow over Woody. 'It's a cowboy dolly . . .'

Back in Andy's room, the toys watched the scene with horror. Buzz looked through the binoculars. 'No, no, no . . .'

'That's not her toy!' Rex shouted.

'What does that little girl think she's

doing?' Slinky demanded.

The girl picked up Woody and ran to her mother. 'Mummy, can we keep him? Please?'

'Oh, honey, we're not going to buy any broken toys,' her mother said, staring at Woody's limp arm. She took Woody from her daughter and put him on a nearby table.

Mrs Davis didn't notice, but someone else did. A tall, thin man with a bushy moustache gasped and ran over to Woody. 'Original hand-painted face, natural dyed blanket-stitched vest . . .' He picked up Woody and grinned. 'Hhmmm, a little rip . . . fixable. Oh, if only you had your hand-stitched polyvinyl . . .' He started to put Woody back on the table, when he spotted Woody's hat.

He stuck Woody's hat back on his head and gave a yelp. 'Hat! Oh, I found him! I found him! I found him!'

Mrs Davis walked across to the man. 'Excuse me. Can I help you?' she asked.

He looked up. 'Oh, ah, I'll give you, ah, fifty cents for all this junk.'

'Oh, now how did this get here?' said Mrs Davis, reaching for Woody.

'Oh, a pro,' the man laughed. 'Very well . . . five dollars.'

'I'm sorry.' Mrs Davis shook her head.

'It's an old family toy.' She took Woody from the man and began to walk away.

He got out his wallet and followed Mrs Davis. 'Wait! Wait! I'll give you fifty bucks for him!' he said, waving the cash in front of Mrs Davis.

'It's not for sale,' she answered.

'Everything's for sale,' the man said wheedlingly. 'Or, or trade . . . Ummm, you like my watch?'

'Sorry,' said Mrs Davis, shaking her head. She put Woody in the cash box and locked it.

The man lurked around outside the yard sale, waiting for the perfect moment when Mrs Davis would be distracted. When she turned her back, he pried open the cash box and grabbed Woody. Hiding Woody in his suitcase, he ran to his car. He dropped the bag in the back seat through an open window, jumped into the car and took off . . . tyres screeching, as he tore down the street.

Woody was being bounced around inside the suitcase. Shaken and terrified, he wondered how he was going to get back to Andy.

Woody heard the car stop and the door open, and then he was lifted out. He

unzipped the bag and peered out. He noticed
a sign and shuddered.

The sign read: NO CHILDREN
ALLOWED.

CHAPTER SEVEN

Back in Andy's room, the toys gathered around to plan a rescue. Hamm paced back and forth in front of Etch.

'All right,' he said. 'Let's review this one more time.' He tapped his pointer on the Etch-A-Sketch, where Woody's figure was drawn. 'At precisely eight thirty-two-ish, Exhibit "A", Woody, was kidnapped. The composite sketch of the kidnapper . . .'

Etch quickly erased Woody, then drew a short fat guy with a beard that almost touched his feet, it was so long.

'He didn't have a beard like that,' Bo protested.

'Fine,' said Hamm. 'Etch, give him a shave.'

Etch erased the man, and drew another one, this time without the beard.

'The kidnapper was bigger than that,' said Slinky.

'I know he wore glasses,' said Bo.

'Yeah, he's too small,' the other toys agreed.

'Oh, picky, picky, picky,' complained Hamm.

'Just go straight to Exhibit "F"!' said an impatient Mr Potato Head.

Exhibit 'F' was a street and traffic scene constructed out of Lincoln Logs. Pointing to a matchbox car, Mr Potato Head traced the route of the car. 'The kidnapper's vehicle fled the scene in this direction.'

'Your eyes are on backwards,' said Hamm. 'It went the other way.'

'Excuse me. A little quiet please,' said Buzz. He was studying Mr Spell, whose screen was lit up with the letters: 'LZTYBRN'.

The toys approached Buzz. 'What are you doing?' Rex asked.

'I managed to catch the licence plate of the car Woody was taken in. There's some sort of message encoded on that vehicle's ID tag.'

Mr Spell gave some suggestions. 'Lazy, Toy, Brain. Lousy, Try, Brian. Liz, Try Bran.

'It's just a licence plate . . . it's just a

jumble of letters,' said Mr Potato Head.

'Yeah, and there are about three point five million registered cars in the tri-county area alone,' said Hamm, turning back to the Etch-A-Sketch.

'Lazy, Try, Brian,' Mr Spell continued.

'Oh, this can't help. Let's just leave Buzz to play with his toys,' said Mr Potato Head.

The other toys started to retreat, when Buzz cracked the code.

'Toy, toy, toy!' he shouted.

'Al's Toy Barn,' said Mr Spell.

'Al's Toy Barn!' they all repeated.

Buzz spun around and ran to Etch. 'Draw that man in the chicken suit!' he said.

When Etch finished the drawing, the toys stared in amazement. 'It's the chicken man!' Rex gasped.

'That's our guy,' said Buzz.

'I knew there was something I didn't like about that chicken!' said Hamm.

CHAPTER EIGHT

Al stamped into his apartment in full chicken-suit gear. He grabbed his mobile phone and started shouting into it. 'Yeah, yeah, yeah. I'll be right there. And we're gonna do this commercial in one take, do you hear me? Because I am in the middle of something really important!' He hung up, and stared at Woody, who was now trapped behind a glass case.

'You, my little cowboy friend, are going to make me big . . .' he began to flap his wings. 'Buck, buck, bucks,' he finished, laughing. It was the laugh of a scary maniac!

When Al left the room, Woody rammed his shoulder into the door of the case. After a few pushes, he was able to open it. He jumped to the floor and rushed across to the door. The door knob was way out of reach, and he couldn't open it. Instead, he jumped up, first on to a chair and then on to the windowsill.

Woody gasped when he got a glimpse outside. There were tall buildings everywhere, and it was clear that he was far from home. 'Andy,' he sighed wistfully.

Woody jumped down from the windowsill and began to explore Al's apartment. Suddenly, a floppy toy horse slipped between his legs. 'Whoa-oa-oa!' shouted Woody, as the horse leapt around like a bucking bronco. Woody struggled to hang on. 'Hey, stop! Horsey, stop! Sit, boy! Whoa! Sit, I say!'

The horse sat down, causing Woody to tumble on to the floor. His legs flipped over his head.

It was when he was upside down that he noticed a cowgirl doll standing in front of him. 'Yeehaw!' she shouted, and grabbed Woody. 'It's you! It's you!' She gave him a big hug. 'It's really you!'

'What's me?' asked Woody.

'Whoo-wee!' exclaimed the cowgirl. She spun Woody around like a square dancer, holding on to his pull string. She yanked him back and caught him with her other arm. Then she put her ear to his chest to listen. 'There's a snake in my boot!' said Woody's voice-box.

'Ha!' said the cowgirl, slapping Woody on the back. 'It is you!'

'Please stop saying that,' Woody pleaded. 'What is going on here?'

'Say hello to Prospector,' said the cowgirl.

She whistled to the horse, who dived into a cardboard box, dug around, and pulled out an old miner doll, still wrapped in his own original plastic casing.

'You remember the Prospector, don't you?' she asked.

'Oh, we've waited countless years for this day! It's so good to see you, Woody,' said the Prospector, who was dressed in mining clothes and had a plastic pick hanging from his belt.

'Listen, I don't know what . . . Hey! How did you know my name?' asked Woody.

'Everyone knows your name, Woody,' said the cowgirl.

'You mean, you don't know who we are?' asked the Prospector. 'Bullseye?' he said.

Bullseye the horse galloped up on to the boxes and turned on the lights.

Woody glanced around the room and gasped. He was surrounded by the complete set: 'Woody's Round-up Collection'.

There were boxes of toys: a tractor, the horse, and an entire ranch. There was a Woody yo-yo, a cereal box, and even a *Time* Magazine cover with a close-up of Woody's face.

Prospector nodded at Bullseye, and the horse pushed a tape into the video. The cowgirl turned on the TV with the remote control. A pair of barn doors flashed on to the screen. The title-card read 'Cowboy Crunchies Presents'.

The TV announcer boomed, 'Cowboy Crunchies, the only cereal that's sugar-frosted and dipped in chocolate, proudly presents . . . Woody's Round-up, starring Jessie! The yodelling cowgirl.'

On screen, a doll just like the cowgirl danced on to the screen. 'Yo-de-lay-he-hoo!' she bellowed.

A mass of animals fell from the sky – skunks, rabbits, armadillos, a squirrel – surrounding Jessie. They squealed and squeaked.

'Look! That's me,' shouted the cowgirl in the room. She jumped up and down and pointed enthusiastically at the screen.

Woody stared from the screen Jessie to the one beside him, confused.

The TV announcer continued: 'The

sharpest horse in the West . . .' as Bullseye galloped on screen.

'Stinky Pete, the Prospector!' On screen, the Prospector emerged from a cardboard mine. 'Has anyone seen my pick?' he asked.

The Prospector smiled at Woody. 'The best is yet to come,' he whispered, nodding to the screen.

'And the high-ridin'est rootin' tootin'est hero of all time – Sheriff Woody!'

Woody watched as his on-stage self burst forward, leapt on to Bullseye and reared up.

'Hey howdy hey, Sheriff Woody,' the audience of kids on screen shouted. Dozens of them were wearing cowboy hats, waving and cheering at their hero.

As the facts came together, Woody's shock turned to joy. He had once been a big TV star.

CHAPTER NINE

Back at Andy's house, the toys had gathered around the TV. They went from channel to channel, searching for the Al's Toy Barn commercial. When they finally found it, Etch quickly sketched a copy of the map, placing a bold 'X' on the spot that marked the Toy Barn.

'That's where I need to go!' Buzz announced, pointing at the X.

'You can't go alone,' said Rex. 'You'll never make it there.'

'Woody once risked his life to save me. I couldn't call myself his friend if I weren't willing to do the same,' Buzz explained. 'So who's with me?' He glanced around the room.

Mrs Potato Head filled Mr Potato Head's rear compartment with attachments. 'I'm packing you an extra pair of shoes, and your *angry* eyes, just in case,' she said to him.

Bo grabbed Buzz and kissed him on the cheek. 'This is for Woody – when you find him,' she said.

Buzz blushed. 'All right, but I don't think it'll mean the same . . . coming from me.'

Slinky, Mr Potato Head, Rex, Buzz and Hamm walked across the rooftop towards the edge. Mr Potato Head grabbed the end of Slinky's coil and jumped off the roof, using Slinky as a bungee rope. 'Geronimo!' he shouted as he landed safely on the lawn below.

Hamm jumped next, and then Rex. Buzz walked back to the window. 'We'll be back before Andy gets home,' he told the others.

The toys inside gathered at the window and waved goodbye. 'To Al's Toy Barn – and beyond!' Buzz shouted as he leapt off the roof. Slinky jumped last. The search for Woody had begun!

CHAPTER TEN

Woody walked around Al's apartment in awe. 'I can't believe I had my own show!' he marvelled. Jessie and Bullseye followed him around. Prospector watched from his box in the corner.

'Didn'cha know? Why, you're valuable property!' said Jessie.

'Oh, I wish the guys could see this. Hey howdy hey, that's me! I'm a yo-yo!' he said, picking up the yo-yo with his face on it and giving it a spin. Next he walked over to 'Woody's Ball Toss' and threw a ball, knocking out his front teeth. He put some coins in the Round-up Bank, and then played with the bubble machine. 'What . . . you push the hat, and out comes . . . Oh, out come bubbles. Clever.' Woody was getting used to the idea of being a star, and he liked it.

Bullseye popped the bubbles with his mouth as they came out. Jessie laughed.

Woody continued to explore, picking up a boot. He looked inside, and a spring snake jumped out, smacking him in the face. 'Ah-ha, I get it! There's a snake in my boot.'

'Check this out, Woody,' said Jessie. She switched on the Woody record-player, and it cranked out old Western music. Bullseye and Jessie began to dance around, and Woody joined them. 'Hop on, cowgirl!' said Woody, as he jumped on to the record-player. The record spun him around and he jumped up to avoid the needle arm. Jessie joined him, jumping in time. 'Not bad,' said Woody.

'Wooo-eee!' shouted Jessie. 'Look at us! We're a complete set!'

'Now it's on to the museum,' said Prospector.

'Museum?' Woody repeated. He stopped short, so that they all tripped over the needle of the record-player. They flew across the room and landed in a heap on the shelf. 'What museum?' Woody groaned.

'We're being sold to the Konishi Toy Museum in Tokyo,' Prospector explained.

'That's in Japan!' Jessie added.

'Japan? I can't go to Japan,' said Woody,

standing up and brushing the dust from his knees.

'What do you mean?' Jessie asked, straightening her pigtails.

'I gotta get back home to my owner – Andy. Look, see?' Woody raised his boot and pointed to the name, 'Andy', which was etched on his sole.

'You still have an owner?' Jessie gasped.

'Oh my goodness . . .' said Prospector, scratching his head.

'I can't do storage again. I won't go back into the dark,' Jessie muttered, pacing back and forth.

'Jessie, it's OK!' said Prospector, as Jessie started to wave her arms frantically, working herself up into a frenzy.

'What's the matter? What's wrong with her?' Woody asked.

Jessie was now crying in the corner.

Prospector explained. 'Well, we've been waiting in storage for a long time, Woody. Waiting for you.'

'Why me?' Woody wanted to know.

'The museum's only interested in the collection if you're in it, Woody. Without you, we go back into storage. It's that simple.'

'It's not fair!' Jessie cried. 'How can you do this to us?'

'Hey, look.' Woody put his arms up and backed away. 'I'm sorry, but this is all a big mistake. See, I was in this yard sale and . . .'

'Yard sale?' said Prospector. 'Why were you in a yard sale if you have an owner?'

'Oh, I wasn't supposed to be there,' Woody explained.

'Is it because you're damaged? Did this Andy break you?' Prospector asked.

Woody cradled his arm in defence. 'Yes, but . . . no, no, no . . . it was an accident. He . . .'

'Sounds like he really loves you,' Jessie snapped.

'It's not like that, OK!' Woody shouted. 'I'm not going to any museum.'

Suddenly the door creaked open. 'Al's coming,' Prospector warned them. The Round-up Gang scrambled to their original positions.

Seconds later, Al was in the room. He bent down and took a Polaroid camera out of a box. 'Oh, ho, ho, ho . . . Money, baby,' Al laughed. He pulled out Bullseye and Jessie and arranged them in front of the Round-up Barn for a shot. 'Money, money, money. And now, the main attraction.' He lifted Woody from his case. But Woody's arm got caught on the stand and it tore off. Al noticed this only after he had sat Woody down on the stand. 'Aaaaah! His arm. Where's his arm?' he shouted.

Al found it on the ground, picked it up, and tried to re-attach it to Woody's shoulder. 'What am I going to do?' he asked. 'Oh, I know.'

Al put Woody down on a chair and then reached for the phone.

'Hey, it's me – Al. I got an emergency here,' he barked into the phone. 'It's got to be done tonight . . . all right, all right. But first thing in the morning. Grrr.' Al slammed the phone down and stamped out of the room, slamming the door behind him.

Woody came back to life. 'It's gone!' he said, horrified. 'I can't believe it. My arm is completely gone!'

'Awright, come here,' said Prospector. 'Let me see that. Oh, it's just a popped seam. You should consider yourself lucky.'

'Lucky! Are you shrink-wrapped?' said Woody. 'I'm missing my arm!'

Jessie slumped in one corner. 'Let him go. I'm sure his precious Andy is dying to play with a one-armed cowboy doll.'

'Why, Jessie,' Prospector said reasonably, 'you know he wouldn't last an hour out there in his condition. It's a dangerous world out there for a toy.'

CHAPTER ELEVEN

Buzz leapt out of a bush, sneaking between pools of light cast by street-lamps. Finally he took cover behind a mailbox at the corner. He looked back and motioned to the others to follow him.

Rex jumped out of the bush first, camouflaged in leaves. As he ran to Buzz, all but one of the leaves fell to the ground. 'Oh,' he laughed, 'this is just like when my invisibility shield wore off on Level Fourteen . . . I was completely exposed! Well! I made an earnest attempt to hide . . .'

Slinky, Potato Head and Hamm appeared next, scurrying along quickly. Hamm tripped over a crack and his cork fell out. Coins clattered to the ground. 'Oow. Ooof. All right, nobody look till I get my cork back in!' he cried.

'So then Zurg annihilated me with his Ion Blaster!' Rex continued.

'Oh, not the video game again,' cried Mr Potato Head. He popped his ears out so he wouldn't have to listen to Rex any more.

Buzz looked down at the map. 'Good work, men. One block down and only nineteen more to go,' he said.

'Nineteen!' the other toys cried.

'Are we gonna do this all night? My parts are killing me,' said Mr Potato Head.

Buzz turned to face the toys. 'Come on, fellas. Did Woody give up when Sid had me strapped to a rocket?'

'No!' the others all shouted.

'No! And did he give up when you threw him out of the back of that moving van?' Buzz asked.

'Oh, you had to bring that up,' said Mr Potato Head.

'We have a friend in need and until he's safe in Andy's room we will not rest. Now let's move out!' Buzz marched down the street, and the other toys followed him.

CHAPTER TWELVE

The sun rose over Andy's neighbourhood. Buzz and the gang were still on their way to Al's Toy Barn. 'Hey, Buzz, can we slow down?' asked Hamm. 'May I remind you that some of us are carrying over six dollars in change.'

'Losing health units . . . must . . . rest,' Rex panted.

Buzz stopped and waited for Hamm, Mr Potato Head, Rex and Slinky to catch up with him. 'Is everyone present and accounted for?' he asked.

'Not quite everyone,' said Mr Potato Head.

'Who's behind?' Buzz asked.

'Mine,' said Slinky, whose back end was trailing far behind.

'Hey, guys!' said Hamm. 'Why did the toys cross the road?'

'Not now, Hamm,' said Buzz.

'Ooh! I love riddles. Why?' Rex asked.

'To get to the chicken on the other side!' Hamm answered. He pointed. Al's Toy Barn was directly across the street. A giant chicken loomed in front of it.

'Hurray! The chicken!' Rex shouted.

Horns honked, and a huge truck rumbled by, shooting a crushed drink can towards the toys.

They ducked and scrambled out of the way. Rex stared at the busy road in front of them and shivered. 'Oh well, we tried,' he said, inching away from the street.

Buzz grabbed him by the tail. 'We'll have to cross,' he said.

'You're not turning me into mashed potato!' said Mr Potato Head.

'I may not be a smart dog,' said Slinky. 'But I know what road kill is!'

Buzz surveyed the scene. He spotted some orange traffic-cones and rubbed his hands together. 'I have an idea!'

A minute later, each toy was securely hidden under an orange traffic-cone at the edge of the road.

'OK, here's our chance! Ready, set, go!' The cones began to move across the road.

Some cars sped in front of them. 'Drop!' Buzz warned them. All the cones dropped.

'Go!' he shouted when it was clear. The cones hurried forward. Cars veered out of their way and, before long, they were safely on the other side of the street.

'Good job, troops,' said Buzz. 'We're that much closer to Woody!'

The toys headed towards Al's Toy Barn, not noticing the huge traffic jam that had grown behind them. When they got close to the entrance, they noticed a large sign that read 'CLOSED'.

'Oh no, it's closed!' Slinky cried.

'We're not preschool toys, Slinky. We can read,' said Mr Potato Head.

'Shhh,' said Rex. 'Someone's coming.'

The toys hid under a shopping trolley as a workman approached. He stepped on the black mat in front of the electronic doors and they slid open.

'Hey, Joe, you're late! We've got a ton of toys to unload in the back. Let's get going,' another workman called out from inside the store.

'All right, I'm coming . . . I'm coming,' said Joe.

The toys glanced at one another. Buzz nodded. 'All right, let's go,' he said.

'But the sign says it's closed,' said Rex.

Everyone ignored him, and they all stood

together on the mat. Finally, Rex followed, shaking his head. But nothing happened; the doors remained closed.

'C'mon, open!' said Hamm. But still the doors stayed closed.

'No, no, no,' said Buzz. 'All together.'

The toys watched as he counted to three. 'Now!' Buzz shouted, and all the toys jumped at once. When they landed, the doors whooshed open and they stepped inside.

Al's Toy Barn was huge. Thousands upon thousands of toys lined the walls. 'Whooaa, Nellie . . . How're we gonna find Woody in this place?' Slinky asked.

'Look for Al,' said Buzz. 'We find Al, we find Woody. Now move out!'

The toys scattered in search of Woody.

Buzz turned a corner and came face to face with an entire aisle of Buzz Lightyear boxes. He stared in awe. 'Wow . . .' He stepped forward to examine the toys more closely. A bright green glow captured his attention. A large cardboard sign read 'Now with utility belt'.

'I could use one of those,' Buzz said in a tone of wonder. He climbed to the top of the display case and reached for the belt. Before he was able to take it, he spotted a giant pair

'Woody's been shelved!'

The other toys watch as Woody is kidnapped!

"It's you!" exclaims Jessie.

A rescue plan is hatched . . .

. . . and the search begins!

Woody can't believe what a big star he was!

Woody teaches Jessie and Bullseye how to play.

'We're being sold to the Konishi Toy Museum in Tokyo,' the Prospector explains.

'I gotta get back home to my owner – Andy. Look, see?'

'Go!' Buzz shouts.

New Buzz begins to scale the walls.

'See, that's me!' says Woody.

'You – are – a – toy!' Buzz exclaims.

'It's Zurg!'
Rex shouts.

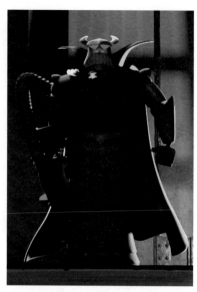

The chase is on!

of moon boots. He glanced up. Towering over him was the new Buzz Lightyear.

Rex and Mr Potato Head were exploring a different aisle. Mr Potato Head had already removed his ears because of Rex's constant talking. 'You know,' said Rex, 'they make it so you can't defeat Zurg unless you buy this book. It's extortion, that's what it is . . .'

A red car zoomed along the aisle towards Rex and Mr Potato Head. It screeched to a halt beside them, revealing its driver and passenger, Hamm and Slinky.

'Eh, I thought we could search in style,' said Hamm.

'Nice going there, Hamm. So, how 'bout letting a toy with fingers drive?' said Mr Potato Head.

Hamm moved over, and Mr Potato Head took the steering wheel. They drove off, ramming into the occasional shelf. Rex continued to babble on about the book he was holding, but no one paid any attention to him.

Old Buzz circled the New Buzz, sizing him up. He checked out his own reflection in New Buzz's shiny helmet glass. 'Am I really that fat?' he wondered. Old Buzz spied the utility belt and reached for it.

'Ho-Yahhh!' shouted New Buzz, forcing Old Buzz's arm into an armlock.

'Oww! What are you doing?' Old Buzz complained.

'You're in direct violation of code six four oh four point five, stating all Space Rangers are to be in hyper-sleep until awakened by authorized personnel,' New Buzz barked in a stiff, computer-like voice.

'Oh no,' said Old Buzz.

New Buzz spun Old Buzz around, pushing him up against the display. 'You're breaking ranks, Ranger,' he said. He opened his wrist communicator. 'Buzz Lightyear to Star Command. I've got an AWOL Space Ranger.'

'Tell me I wasn't this deluded,' Old Buzz complained, rolling his eyes.

'No back talk,' New Buzz warned him. 'I have a laser and I will use it.'

'You mean the laser that's a light bulb?' Old Buzz teased him as he pressed the laser.

New Buzz gasped. 'Has your mind been melded? You could've killed me, Space Ranger. Or should I say, "Traitor"?'

Old Buzz broke free. 'I don't have time for this,' he said.

New Buzz raised his laser and aimed it

46

at Old Buzz's head. 'Halt! I order you to halt!'

Old Buzz dropped from the podium to the floor. New Buzz jumped on his back, tackling him. They began to wrestle. Old Buzz pushed New Buzz into the Buzz Lightyear Pin Screen.

Hamm, Potato Head, Slinky and Rex were driving along the Barbie aisle. 'We've been down this aisle already,' said Slinky.

'We've never been down this aisle, it's pink!' said Mr Potato Head.

'Face it, we're lost,' said Slinky.

'Back it up, back it up,' said Hamm.

The toys stopped and backed up in front of the Barbie Beach Party. Barbie and her friends were limbo dancing. 'How low can ya go? How low can ya go?' they chanted.

'Excuse me, ladies,' Hamm interrupted them. 'Does anyone know where we might find the Al of Al's Toy Barn?'

'I can help,' said another Barbie doll. She slid down a slide and jumped into the driver's seat. 'I'm Tour Guide Barbie! Please keep your hands, arms and accessories inside the car, and no flash photography. Thank you!'

Barbie smiled at Mr Potato Head, who

closed his eyes and whispered, 'I'm a married spud. I'm a married spud.'

Hamm pushed him aside. 'Then make room for the single fellas!' he said, sitting down next to Barbie. The car sped off.

'To our right is the Hot Wheels aisle. Developed in nineteen sixty-seven, the original series had sixteen cars, including the Corvette.'

'Uh, beg your pardon, ma'am,' Slinky interrupted her. 'But where's Al's office?'

'Please hold all questions until the end of the tour. Thank you,' Barbie replied.

Rex read from his 'Defeat Zurg' manual. 'Wow! It says how you defeat Zurg! Look!' Rex placed the book in front of Barbie's face, completely blocking her view. The car swerved, and the other toys screamed.

'Rex! Watch it! Look out! We can't see!' they shouted.

The car was heading straight for a giant box of super balls. 'Look out!' Slinky shouted.

Barbie was able to regain control of the wheel by swerving at the last minute. She grazed the side of the box, and the super balls spilled out, cascading wildly to the ground and creating a blizzard of multi-coloured rubber. Balls bounced off everything, including the car, Mr Potato Head and Hamm. Everyone shouted, as the car spun around wildly.

'Turn into the spin, Barbie!' said Hamm.

Rex's Zurg manual flew out of the car. 'My source of power!' he shouted, jumping out of the car and chasing after the book. It slid under a shelf, lost. 'Where'd it go? No! Come back!' He watched the car speed away. 'Wait up! Dinosaur overboard!' Rex raced after the car.

Barbie stopped short and Rex ran straight into the car. 'For your safety, please remain seated at all times. *Permanez ca stendados por favor*,' said Barbie.

Meanwhile, Old Buzz had been overtaken by New Buzz. New Buzz shoved Old Buzz into an empty box, and used packaging wires to secure him.

'Ow!' said Old Buzz. 'Listen to me! You're not really a Space Ranger! You're a toy! We're all toys! Do you hear me?'

New Buzz closed the cardboard container. 'Well, that should hold you until the court martial!'

'Let me go!' Old Buzz pleaded from the box.

New Buzz was turning to leave just as

Barbie and the toys pulled up to him in the car.

Barbie pointed. 'And this is the Buzz Lightyear aisle. Back in nineteen ninety-five, short-sighted retailers did not order enough dolls to meet demand.'

'Hey, Buzz,' said Hamm.

New Buzz turned, took aim, and fired his laser at the toys. 'Halt!' he shouted. 'Who goes there?'

'Quit clowning around and get in the car,' said Mr Potato Head.

'Buzz! Buzz! I know how to defeat Zurg!' said Rex.

'You do?' asked New Buzz.

'C'mon, I'll tell you about it on the way,' said Rex.

Old Buzz watched from the shelf, horrified. 'No, no, guys! You've got the wrong Buzz!'

'Say, where did ya get that cool belt, Buzz?' Hamm asked.

'Well, slotted pig, they're standard issue,' said New Buzz. He got in the car and they drove away.

Old Buzz was still shouting from the box, but no one could hear him.

CHAPTER THIRTEEN

A flash went off, blinding Woody momentarily. He was propped up on his stand, the rest of the Round-up Gang set up around him. Flash, flash, flash . . .

Al fanned through his new Polaroids, a huge smile on his face. 'It's like printing my own money!' he exclaimed. The phone rang and Al picked it up. 'Yeah, what?' he shouted. 'Oh, oh, Mr Konishi. I have the pictures right here. In fact, I'm in the car right now, on my way to the office to fax them to you. I'm going through the tunnel,' he lied. 'I'm breaking up.' He made some garbled sounds and then disconnected the phone.

As soon as Al left the room, Woody leapt from his stand. 'Oh wow! Will you look at me! It's like I'm fresh out of the box!' Woody admired his fixed arm; someone had come to sew it on and clean him up. He admired his new stitching. 'Will you look at this! Andy's gonna have a hard time ripping this!' Woody waved his new arm about in front of the other toys' faces. 'Hello! Hi! Hello!'

Woody admired his reflection in the cellophane of the Prospector's box.

Jessie frowned and walked away. 'Great, now you can go,' she said coldly.

'Well, what a good idea,' said Woody. He walked to the edge of the table and looked at the heating grate below. Bullseye nudged him from behind and Woody turned, staring into Bullseye's sad eyes.

'Woody, don't be mad at Jessie,' said Prospector. 'She's been through more than you know. Why not make amends before you leave, huh? It's the least you can do.'

Woody sighed. 'All right. But I don't know what good it'll do.'

He went over to Jessie, who was hugging her knees and staring out of the window.

'Look, Jessie. I know you hate me for leaving, but I have to go back. I'm still Andy's toy. Well, if you knew him, you'd understand. You see, Andy's a real —'

'Let me guess,' Jessie interrupted. 'Andy's a real special kid, and, to him, you're his buddy, his best friend; and when Andy plays with you, it's like, even though you're not moving, you feel like you're alive – because that's how he sees you.'

'How did you know?' Woody asked. He was truly stunned.

Jessie stared at Woody. 'Because Emily was just the same. She was my whole world.' Jessie started to cry and buried her head in her hands. Her voice came out muffled. 'You never forget kids like Emily, or Andy, but they forget you,' she sobbed.

'Jessie, I . . . I didn't know,' said Woody.

'Just go,' she said.

Woody reluctantly walked away. He jumped off the windowsill on to the floor and went back to the grate where the Prospector and Bullseye were standing. Woody opened the grate and stared down at the ventilation shaft. He glanced back at Jessie.

'How long will it last, Woody?' Prospector asked. 'Do you really think Andy is going to take you to college? Or on his honeymoon? Andy's growing up and there's nothing you can do about it. It's your choice, Woody. You can go back, or you can stay with us and be adored by children for generations. You'll live for ever.'

Woody let go of the grate and spun

around. 'Who am I to break up the Round-up Gang?' he said.

Bullseye licked his hand, and Prospector smiled. Woody and Jessie grinned broadly at each other.

CHAPTER FOURTEEN

The toys were rummaging through the desk drawers at Al's office.

'Woody, are you in here?' Hamm asked.

'Woody?' they called.

Rex approached New Buzz. 'You see, all along we thought that the way into Zurg's fortress was through the main gate. But in fact the secret entrance is to the left, hidden in the shadows.'

'To the left and in the shadows. Got it,' said New Buzz.

They heard Al enter the office and they all hid.

Al turned on his fax machine while he was talking into his mobile phone. 'Yeah, there was a big pile up, but I don't want to bore you with the details. Now let me confirm your fax number. All right, slower.

That's a lot of numbers. I got it.'

'It's him,' Slinky whispered.

'The chicken man,' said Hamm.

'Funny, he doesn't look like poultry,' said New Buzz.

'That's the kidnapper, all right,' said Slinky.

'An agent of Zurg if I ever saw one,' said New Buzz.

Al slid a Polaroid of Woody through the fax. 'And the *pièce de résistance* . . . I promise the collection will be the crown jewel of your museum!' The photo went through the machine and popped out on the other side, falling to the floor near the hiding toys.

'Woody!' they gasped.

'Now that I have your attention, imagine we added another zero to the price, huh? What? Yes? Yes! You've got a deal!' Al shouted. 'I'll be on the next flight to Japan!'

'He's selling Woody to a toy museum,' Mr Potato Head whispered.

'In Japan!' said Rex.

New Buzz pushed everyone into Al's bag. 'Into the poultry man's cargo unit. He'll lead us to Zurg. Move, move, move!'

Al was laughing like a maniac. 'You're gonna be rich! Rich! Rich!' he bellowed, picking up his bag as the last of the toys slipped in. Rex's tail was hanging out of the back of the bag, but Al didn't notice.

CHAPTER FIFTEEN

Back at the toy store, Old Buzz had managed to shift the box he was in sideways on the shelf. Each shove against the plastic moved him another inch until he was teetering over the edge and he finally dropped to the floor. He kicked open the bottom of the box, then struggled with the arm restraints. He jerked his right arm hard and broke free. Untying the rest of his body, he crawled out of the box, kicking it in disgust.

Old Buzz heard Al coming along the aisle and he hid. Peering around the corner after Al turned, he noticed Rex's tail sticking out of the back of the bag that Al carried. Old Buzz raced along the aisle, trying to catch up with his friends. He was almost there when he slipped on some super balls, left loose after Barbie's crash. Buzz recovered quickly and crawled up a display case. Swinging like a gymnast, he jumped on to a trampoline.

When he was bouncing high enough, Buzz dived towards the closing electric doors in desperation . . . and smacked right into the glass. 'Ooph!' Buzz shouted. He jumped up and down on the electric sensor, but the door just wouldn't budge. Looking around, Buzz spotted a large stack of boxes by the door. He kicked out the bottom box out, so that the entire pile toppled over. The door opened with their weight, and Buzz ran towards it. Standing in his way was a Zurg box, and Buzz stopped to place it upright. Then Old Buzz ran out through the door, chasing after Al.

Buzz didn't notice that when the electronic doors closed, the top of Zurg's box ripped open. Zurg crawled out, and his head whipped towards Buzz. His red eyes glowed and his claws clenched as he watched Buzz. His deep mechanical voice growled, 'Destroy Buzz Lightyear . . . Destroy Buzz Lightyear.' Having been set free, Zurg followed Buzz's trail.

CHAPTER SIXTEEN

The toys heard the car engine stop and Al get out, slamming the door behind him.

Rex peered out. 'He didn't take the bag!' he said, as he watched from inside.

New Buzz hopped over Rex and jumped out. 'No time to lose,' he said. He tried the door handle but couldn't get it open.

They all watched Al get into the lift. 'He's ascending in the vertical transporter,' said New Buzz. He opened his wings and grabbed hold of Rex and Mr Potato Head. 'All right, everyone! Hang on! We're going to blast through the roof!'

'Uh, Buzz,' said Rex.

'To infinity and beyond!' Buzz boomed.

'What are you, insane?' Mr Potato Head asked. He noticed that there was a door lock next to the window, and he ran up Rex's back so he could reach it. 'Stand still, Godzilla,' he said. Mr Potato Head strained to lift the lock.

New Buzz scratched his head and leant against the electric window switch. 'I don't understand. Somehow my fuel cells have gone dry . . .'

Ka-chunk! Suddenly the lock popped open, tearing off Mr Potato Head's arms. He sailed through the air and bounced off Slinky's head. 'Ahhh!' he shouted, finally landing, upside down, in the cup holder.

The car door opened and New Buzz ran out. He watched through the glass doors as the lift's indicator stopped at the penthouse. 'Blast!' New Buzz cried. 'He's on Level Twenty-three.'

'How are we gonna get up there?' Slinky asked.

Rex looked up. 'Maybe if we found some balloons, we could float to the top . . .'

The others looked at him in surprise. 'Are you kidding?' Mr Potato Head asked. 'I say we stack ourselves up, push the intercom, and pretend we're delivering a pizza!'

'How about a ham sandwich?' Hamm suggested. He glanced at Mr Potato Head and Slinky. 'With fries and a hot dog?'

'What about me?' Rex asked.

'Eh, you can be the toy that comes with the meal,' Hamm said, shrugging.

'Troops! Over here,' said New Buzz.

They all turned to see New Buzz taking the cover off an air vent. 'Just like you said, Lizard Man – in the shadows, to the left. OK, let's move!'

The toys followed New Buzz into the vent. New Buzz spoke into his wrist communicator. 'Mission Log – have infiltrated enemy territory without detection and are making our way through the bowels of Zurg's fortress.'

Hamm turned to the others. 'You know, I think that Buzz aisle went to his head,' he whispered. The others nodded, but that didn't stop them following him through the shaft.

They soon came to a crossroads. Slinky looked in both directions. 'Oh no . . . which way do we go?' he asked.

'This way,' said New Buzz, running forward.

'What makes you so sure?' Mr Potato Head wanted to know.

'I'm Buzz Lightyear. I'm always sure!'

A noise echoed throughout the duct. 'We've been detected,' said New Buzz. 'The walls! They're closing in.' New Buzz grabbed

Mr Potato Head and lifted him over his head. 'Quick! Help me prop up Vegetable Man, or we're done for!' he said.

'Put me down, you moron!' Mr Potato Head cried.

'Hey, guys, look! It's not the walls, it's the lift,' said Rex. He pointed to a different vent where they caught sight of the lift descending.

They walked across to the lift shaft and peered up. New Buzz put on his suction-cup gloves and reeled out a line with a hook. 'Come on,' he said. 'We've got no time to lose.' He handed out the line. 'Everyone grab hold.'

'Huh?' the others said.

'Hey, uh, Buzz?' Hamm asked. 'Why don't we just take the lift?'

New Buzz began to scale the walls. 'They'll be expecting that,' he explained.

Meanwhile, a weary and frustrated Old Buzz had made it as far as the front of Al's apartment building. He noticed a trail of footprints in the soft grass leading to the vent. He ducked down and followed the trail.

CHAPTER SEVENTEEN

Al paced back and forth in his living room, shouting into his phone once more. 'To overnight six packages to Japan is how much? What? That's in yen, right? Dollars? Doh! You are deliberately taking advantage of people in a hurry, you know that? All right, I don't . . . I'll do it! All right, fine!'

He stacked a bunch of boxes on to a cart with wheels and headed out through the door with it. 'I'll have the stuff waiting in the lobby, and you'd better be here in fifteen minutes, because I have a plane to catch. Do you hear me?'

The Round-up Gang was packed into their boxes. When Al had gone, Woody, Jessie and Bullseye sat up.

'Woo-hoo!' Jessie shouted. 'We're finally

going! Can you believe it?'

Bullseye sniffed excitedly and then snuggled down into his thick foam packaging.

Prospector chuckled. 'That's custom-fitted foam insulation you'll be riding in, Bullseye. First-class stuff, all the way!'

'You know what?' said Woody. 'I'm actually excited about this. I mean it. I really am.'

Jessie jumped next to Woody, and they began to square dance. 'Yee-haw! Swing yer partner, doh-see-doh ... Look at you, dancin' cowboy,' she said.

Bullseye clapped his hoofs. Prospector slid his box back and forth. 'Look! I'm doing the box step!' he cried.

CHAPTER EIGHTEEN

Thock, thock, thock. New Buzz climbed the wall slowly with his suction gloves, pulling the others up behind him.

Hamm grunted. He tilted and some of the change began to drop out of his coin slot. 'Uh-oh . . . Hey, heads up down there,' he called out.

'Whoa! Pork bellies are falling,' said Slinky.

Some coins landed on Mr Potato Head's face. 'Hey,' he shouted. 'Not much further, Buzz?' he asked hopefully.

'My arms can't hold on much longer,' Rex complained. The lift shaft shuddered, causing Rex to slide down the line. He bumped into the other toys and pushed them down with him, until they were all desperately clinging to the bottom of the tow-line.

'Buzz, help!' Slinky called.

'Too . . . heavy . . .' New Buzz panted. 'What was I thinking? My anti-gravity servos!' He pushed a button on his utility belt.

'Hurry up, Buzz,' said Hamm.

'Hang tight, everyone,' said New Buzz. 'I'm going to let go of the wall.'

'What!' all the toys cried.

'He wouldn't,' said Mr Potato Head.

'One,' said Buzz.

'He would,' said Hamm.

'Two,' he called.

'For the love of . . . no!'

'Three,' New Buzz called out. He pushed off from the wall and went into his flying pose. He looked up, his fist jutting forward. They were frozen in space for a second. And then . . . they plummeted down, landing on the top of the lift as it was rising.

'To infinity and beyond,' New Buzz declared, unaware that his attempt at flying had failed.

The lift began to slow down. 'Approaching new destination. Re-engaging gravity,' New Buzz said. The others looked at one another and rolled their eyes.

The lift stopped opposite the airshaft at the twenty-third floor. New Buzz leapt into the vent and scanned about him. 'Area secure,' he reported to the others.

They groaned and panted as they climbed into the vent.

'It's OK, troops. The anti-gravity sickness will wear off momentarily. Now ... let's move!' said Buzz.

'Remind me to glue his helmet shut when we get back,' Mr Potato Head whispered to Hamm.

Once inside the vent, New Buzz spoke into his wrist communicator again. 'Have reached Zurg's command deck, but no sign of him, or his wooden captive.'

Suddenly Woody's voice echoed through the chambers.

'That's Woody!' said Slinky.

The toys turned and ran down the vent. They reached the grating to Al's apartment in a few seconds, and tried to peer through.

Woody was being tickled by Jessie, but his friends could only hear his voice. 'I'm begging you! No more! I'm begging you, stop. Please!' he shouted.

'Buzz, can you see what's going on?' Mr Potato Head asked.

New Buzz lifted Mr Potato Head up to the slats in the vent. 'What's happening?'

Mr Potato Head gasped. 'It's horrible! They're torturing him!'

'What are we going to do, Buzz?' Rex asked.

'Use your head,' said New Buzz.

The toys grabbed Rex and aimed his head at the door. Using him as a battering ram, they scrambled forward. 'But I don't want to use my head,' Rex cried.

'CHARGE!' they all shouted.

Woody had left the grating unscrewed, so the stampeding toys caused it to fall down even before they reached it. Unable to stop, they all sped into the room, passing the Round-up Gang and crashing into the far wall.

Everyone shouted.

'What's going on here?' Prospector asked.

'Guys!' Woody cried. 'Hey, how did you find me?'

'We're here to spring you, Woody,' Slinky explained.

Andy's toys rushed the Round-up Gang.

'Hold it, now! Hey, you don't understand! These are my friends,' said Woody.

'Yeah, we're his friends,' said Rex, puffing his chest out.

'Well, not you – them,' said Woody, nodding at the Round-up Gang.

Slinky quickly circled around Jessie and

Bullseye, tying them up with his coils.

'Hey,' said Jessie.

'Grab Woody and let's go,' said Slinky.

New Buzz ran to Woody, picked him up and started to carry him off.

'Fellas, hold it!' Woody protested. 'Hey, Buzz – put me down.'

'They're stealing him!' Jessie cried.

The toys rushed towards the vent, but Old Buzz was blocking it. 'Hold it right there!' he said.

'Buzz?' said Woody and Andy's other toys.

'You again?' New Buzz asked.

Old Buzz looked up at Woody, who was still in New Buzz's arms. 'Woody, thank goodness you're all right.'

'Buzz, what's going on?' Woody asked.

New Buzz dropped Woody. 'Hold on a minute. I am Buzz Lightyear, and I'm in charge of this detachment.'

'No, I'm Buzz Lightyear,' Old Buzz said to the others.

'So who's the real Buzz?' Woody asked.

'I am,' they both said.

New Buzz turned to the others. 'Don't let this impostor fool you. He's probably been trained by Zurg himself to mimic my every move.'

Old Buzz reached over and popped

New Buzz's helmet open. New Buzz spluttered and gasped for air, falling to the ground.

While New Buzz faltered, Old Buzz calmly lifted his foot and showed everyone the 'ANDY' written on the sole.

'I had a feeling it was you, Buzz,' said Slinky. 'My front end just had to catch up to my back end.'

Rex looked from one Buzz to the other. 'You know, now that I really look, I can see the difference.'

New Buzz managed to close his helmet and stand up. 'Will someone please explain what's going on?' he asked.

'It's all right, Space Ranger,' said Old Buzz. 'It's a code Five-four-six.'

'You mean it's a . . .' said New Buzz.

'Yes,' said Old Buzz.

'And he's a . . .' said New Buzz.

'Yes,' said Old Buzz.

New Buzz rushed over to Woody and bowed down on one knee. 'Your majesty,' he said.

Woody looked down, confused.

Old Buzz took Woody's arm. 'Woody, you're in danger here. We need to leave now.'

'Al's selling you to a toy museum, in Japan!' said Rex.

'I know, it's OK,' said Woody, pulling away. 'I actually want to go.'

'What? Are you crazy?' Mr Potato Head asked.

'The thing is,' Woody explained, 'I'm a rare Sheriff Woody doll, and these guys are my Round-up Gang. He gestured to Jessie, Bullseye and Prospector, who waved.

'What are you talking about?' Mr Potato Head asked.

'Woody's Round-up! It's this great old TV show, and I was the star!'

Woody clicked the remote control, and the TV and video turned on, with the show playing in the middle of an episode.

'See, now look . . . Look at me! See, that's me!' said Woody.

On the screen, the TV Woody was riding the TV Bullseye towards a cliff. TV Jessie fell off, and they caught her.

Andy's toys watched in amazement.

'This is weirdin' me out,' Hamm announced.

Woody explained. 'Buzz, it was a national phenomenon. And there was all this merchandise, you should see it. There was a record-player, a cereal box, and a yo-yo. Buzz, I was a yo-yo.'

'Was?' Mr Potato Head repeated.

Old Buzz pulled Woody aside. 'Woody, stop this nonsense and let's go.'

'I can't go. I can't abandon these guys. Without me the set's incomplete. They'll go back into storage – maybe for ever. They need me to get into the museum.'

Old Buzz raised his voice. 'You – Are – A – Toy! You're not a collector's item. You are a child's plaything.'

'For how much longer?' Woody reasoned with him. 'One more rip, and Andy's done with me. What do I do then, Buzz, huh? You tell me.'

'Woody, the point is being there for Andy when he needs us,' said Old Buzz. 'You taught me that. That's why we came all this way to get you.'

'Well, you wasted your time,' Woody sighed.

Old Buzz and Woody stared at each other for a moment.

Old Buzz turned towards the grating. 'Let's go, everyone,' he said.

'What about Woody?' Slinky asked.

'He's not coming with us,' said Old Buzz.

'But, but, Andy's coming home tonight,' said Rex.

'Then we'd better make sure we're there waiting for him,' said Old Buzz.

Old Buzz held the vent open for the rest of Andy's toys, and New Buzz. They glanced at Woody sadly, before filing out and then disappearing into the darkness. Old Buzz paused.

'I don't have a choice, Buzz,' Woody said, shrugging his shoulders. 'This museum . . . it's my only chance.'

'To do what, Woody?' Old Buzz asked. 'Watch children from behind glass? Some life.'

He jumped into the vent, and closed the grating behind him.

Woody stared at the closed grating as the Round-up toys approached him.

'Good going, Woody. I thought they'd never leave,' said Prospector.

Woody wandered over to the TV to watch the end of the episode. The TV Woody was singing. 'You've got a friend in me. You've got troubles, and I've got 'em too . . . There isn't anything I wouldn't do for you.'

The song trickled in through the grating, and Andy's toys paused to listen for a moment.

On the TV screen, a shy little boy was pushed on to the stage. He approached TV Woody slowly. 'We stick together, and we see it through 'cause, you've got a friend in me,' sang TV Woody. The boy hugged TV Woody with all his might. TV Woody kept singing. 'Some other folks might be a little bit smarter than I am, bigger and stronger too. But none of them will ever love you, the way I do, it's me and you . . .'

Woody looked down at the sole of his shoe. He scratched away the new paint until the name 'Andy' showed through. Woody stood up. 'What am I doing?' he said. He ran past the Round-up Gang, heading straight for the vent.

'W-Woody? Where are you going?' Prospector asked.

'You're right, Prospector. I can't stop Andy from growing up, but I wouldn't miss it for the world!'

'No!' Jessie and Prospector gasped.

'Buzz, Buzz,' Woody shouted, running through the vent.

Both Buzzes turned. 'Yes?' they asked.

'Wait! I'm coming with you!' Woody said.

Andy's toys cheered.

'Wait for me,' said Woody. 'I'll be back in just a second.' He turned on his boot heel and headed back towards Al's apartment.

CHAPTER NINETEEN

Woody rushed back into Al's apartment. 'Hey, you guys!' he called to the Round-up Gang. 'Come with me!'

Jessie, Bullseye and Prospector stared at Woody in surprise.

'Look,' Woody said, 'I know I won't be played with for ever, but Buzz is right. Today I still have Andy, and today I know he'd play with all of us.'

'Woody, I . . . I don't know,' Jessie stuttered.

'Wouldn't you give anything just to have one more day with Emily?' Woody asked. 'Well, well, here's your chance! Come on! Take it!' Woody glanced at Bullseye. 'Are you with me?' he asked.

Bullseye licked Woody's face eagerly.

'Good boy. Good boy. Prospector, how

about you?' Woody turned to Prospector's box, but it was empty!

Woody's eyes opened wide with horror. Prospector had slammed the grating shut and was using his plastic pick like a power tool to spin the screws tight.

Jessie gasped.

'You're outta your box?' Woody asked, horrified.

'I tried reasoning with you, Woody,' said Prospector. He finished tightening the screws and walked back to his box. 'But you keep forcing me to take extreme measures.'

Woody started to protest, but Prospector raised his hand to silence him. 'Look, we have an eternity to spend together in the museum. Let's not start off by pointing fingers, shall we?'

'Prospector! This isn't fair,' said Jessie.

'Fair,' said Prospector. 'I'll tell you what's not *fair*. Spending a lifetime on a dime-store shelf, watching every other toy be sold. Well, finally my waiting has paid off, and no hand-me-down cowboy doll is gonna screw it up for me now!' Prospector flung his box into the special packing case and then climbed in himself.

Woody ran to the vent, pulling on the

grating. 'Help! Help! Buzz! Guys!' he screamed.

'It's too late,' Prospector shouted. 'That silly Buzz Lightweight can't help you.'

'His name is Buzz Lightyear!' Woody shouted.

'Whatever,' said Prospector, closing the lid of his box.

The toys raced down the vent towards the grating. They struggled to open it, but it wouldn't budge.

'It's stuck,' Woody called out to them.

The two Buzzes began slamming into it. 'Should I use my head?' Rex offered.

The lock on Al's apartment door began to rattle. Jessie and Bullseye jumped into their cases as the door creaked open. Woody had no choice but to join the rest of the Round-up Gang.

'Ah! Look at the time. I'm gonna be late,' Al growled.

Andy's toys watched in horror as Woody was taken away.

'Quick! To the lift,' Old Buzz cried.

CHAPTER TWENTY

Riding on top of the lift was Zurg. 'All too easy,' he muttered, as two Buzz Lightyears came into view.

'It's Zurg!' Rex shouted. 'Watch out, he's got an Ion Blaster.'

Zurg fired at New Buzz, who jumped into action. He leapt over Zurg, and moved swiftly to avoid all his assaults.

Zurg whipped his body around and fired his Ion bullets. 'Pop, pop, pop.'

New Buzz ducked for cover behind a generator box.

Meanwhile, Al was getting into the lift, with the Round-up Gang in tow.

As the lift descended, New Buzz and Zurg began a fist fight.

'Quick, get on,' Old Buzz cried. The toys jumped on to the roof of the lift. They watched New Buzz's struggle. Zurg lifted him over his head, and threw him to the ground.

'Surrender, Buzz Lightyear. I have won,' Zurg boomed.

'I'll never give in. You killed my father,' said New Buzz.

'No, Buzz . . . I am your father,' said Zurg.

'NO-O-O!' New Buzz screamed.

Rex scrambled down from the roof of the lift and ran behind Zurg. 'Buzz, you could have defeated Zurg all along. You just need to believe in yourself!' he said.

Zurg raised his blaster to New Buzz's head. 'Prepare to die!' Zurg shouted.

'Ahh, I can't look,' said Rex, covering his eyes. As he turned away, his tail knocked Zurg off balance. Zurg fell, rolled to the edge of the lift shaft and then fell down, plunging into the darkness.

'AAHHHH!' Zurg shouted.

Rex peered over the edge of the lift shaft. 'I did it! I finally defeated Zurg!'

New Buzz joined Rex and looked down. 'Father?'

Meanwhile, Slinky dangled and stretched down into the lift, and eventually managed to unlock Al's case, freeing Woody. They grabbed hold of each other as the lift reached the lobby. Slinky pulled Woody from one end, but Prospector pulled from the other, forcing Woody back into the case.

Al walked out of the lift, taking Woody with him. The toys followed closely behind.

'How are we gonna get him now?' Rex asked.

Mr Potato Head pointed to an idling Pizza Planet Truck. 'Pizza, anyone?' he asked. Everyone smiled and headed towards the truck.

Old Buzz noticed New Buzz falling behind. 'Are you coming?' he asked.

New Buzz was carrying a lifeless Zurg in his arms. 'No. I must bury my father, and fill out the proper forms.' They waved goodbye, and New Buzz walked back to Al's Toy Barn.

The toys climbed into the truck and Old Buzz took control of the situation. 'Slink, take the pedals. Rex, you navigate.' He slid a stack of pizza boxes under the steering wheel. 'Hamm and Potato, operate the levers and knobs.'

Inside the truck, three tiny green aliens hung from the rear-view mirror. 'Strangers, from the outside,' they said.

'Oh no!' Old Buzz cried.

Rex pointed. 'He's at the red light. We can catch him.'

'Maximum power, Slink.' Old Buzz gave the order.

Slinky pushed on the accelerator with all his might. The truck wouldn't budge. On the dashboard, Rex peered through the windscreen. 'It turned green. Hurry up!'

'Why won't it go?' Buzz asked.

The aliens pointed to the gear lever. 'Use the wand of power,' they said.

Standing on top of Hamm, Mr Potato Head struggled to get the car into gear. He jammed the gears hard and the truck shot forward.

'Ahh!' Rex shouted as the truck hit a line of orange traffic-cones.

'Rex, which way?' Old Buzz asked.

'Right. I mean left. No, no, right . . . I mean your right!' said Rex.

The truck sped along the street, swerving wildly from side to side.

Al's car turned. 'There he is!' Rex shouted. 'He's turning left!'

Buzz turned the steering wheel, and the truck cut across three lanes of traffic. The aliens were swinging on a string, and they flew across the car, heading out through the window. Mr Potato Head leant across and grabbed them just in time.

'Buzz! Go right! To the right! Right!' Rex shouted.

The truck turned again, and Mr Potato Head and the aliens whipped back into the truck safely.

'You saved our lives!' the aliens chanted. 'We are for ever in your debt.'

Mr Potato Head slapped his forehead and groaned.

The toys sped into the airport, parking in the unloading area. 'There he is!' said Old Buzz, pointing to Al.

Al was at the ticket counter. 'I'm sorry, sir. We're going to have to check that bag,' said the ticket agent.

'Whoa, what do ya mean you have to check this?' Al asked.

'It won't fit in the overhead,' the ticket agent explained.

'You can't check this. These things are very valuable.'

'Sorry, sir,' said the ticket agent.

'It has to remain with me at all times,' Al argued.

The ticket agent shook her head and lifted Al's case on to the conveyor belt behind her.

The toys sneaked up behind Al, hidden in

a pet carrier. 'Once we get through, we just need to find that case,' said Buzz. The pet carrier was checked in, and the toys rode down the conveyor belt with the bags. When the carrier tumbled on to the lower conveyor belt, it burst open, freeing the toys.

Slinky spied Al's case first. 'There it is!' he shouted, pointing to the right.

'No, there's the case!' said Hamm, pointing to the left.

'You take that one, and we'll take this one,' said Buzz.

Hamm and Mr Potato Head ran to the case on the left. They unzipped it, only to find a jumble of camera equipment.

Buzz chased after the bag on the right and kicked open the latch. 'OK, Woody, let's go!' he called. Buzz opened the case and reached into it, only to be punched and knocked off the belt by Prospector.

Prospector climbed out and waved his plastic pick at Buzz. 'Take that, space toy!'

Woody suddenly popped up beside Prospector and grabbed him in a headlock. 'Hey! No one does that to my friend!'

In their struggle, both toys fell out of the case. Prospector slashed Woody's arm with his pick, and it ripped open once again.

'Your choice, Woody!' Prospector growled.

'You can go to Japan together . . . or in pieces! If he fixed you once, he can fix you again! Now get in the box.'

'Never,' said Woody.

Prospector raised his pick in order to land one final blow when he was suddenly blinded by light.

'Snap, snap, snap.' Andy's toys took shots of Prospector with the cameras, distracting him with the flashing.

'Gotcha!' Buzz shouted, grabbing Prospector.

'Fools!' Prospector spluttered. 'Children will destroy you! You'll be ruined! Forgotten! Thrown away . . . spending eternity decomposing in some rotten landfill!'

'Well, Stinky Pete, I think it's time you learned the true meaning of "playtime",' said Woody. 'Right over there, guys.'

'No!' Prospector gasped, as they stuffed him into a Hello Kitty Backpack. 'You can't do this to me! Noooo!'

'Hi!' said a Barbie doll. Prospector looked up, startled. He turned the other way to find another Barbie.

'You'll like Amy,' said the second Barbie doll. 'She's an artist.'

Prospector was surrounded by six Barbie dolls in various states of design. Scattered in the bag with them were crayons, scissors and paint brushes.

Prospector screamed as the bag made its way along on the conveyor belt.

Buzz and Woody waved. 'Happy trails, Prospector,' Woody called after him.

'Hey, Woody,' said Hamm. 'We can't get Jessie out.' The case was approaching the end of the line, and Jessie was stuck inside.

'Woody! Help!' she shouted. Still in the case, Jessie plummeted down a steep ramp. The toys watched in horror as a baggage-handler closed the case, loaded it on to a truck, and drove off.

Woody whistled and Bullseye galloped forward. Woody and Buzz jumped on his back.

'Ride like the wind, Bullseye,' Woody shouted.

Bullseye reared up and took off in pursuit of Jessie.

'Yee-ha! Giddy-up!' Woody cried.

The three sidled up, next to the suitcase. Woody jumped on to the truck and struggled with the case. The baggage-handlers approached, and Woody had to freeze, watching in horror as the case was loaded on to a plane.

Woody managed to sneak on to the plane.

He found the bag and opened it, finding Jessie on top of the foam. 'Excuse me, ma'am . . . but I believe you're on the wrong flight.'

'Woody!' Jessie shouted.

'Come on, Jess. It's time to take you home.' Woody hugged Jessie.

'But I'm a girl toy,' said Jessie.

'Nonsense,' said Woody. 'Andy will love you. Besides, he's got a little sister.'

'He does?' said Jessie. 'Well, why didn't you say so? Let's go.'

Woody took Jessie's arm and pulled her out of the case. The two ran behind a suitcase, hiding from the baggage-handler.

Before they could escape though, the doors closed.

From the runway below, Buzz and Bullseye stared in disbelief.

'What are we gonna do?' Jessie gasped.

'Come on! Over there!' Woody pointed to some light that was leaking in at the other end of the cargo hold. They ran over and peered through the opening, at the landing gear below.

'Are you sure about this?' Jessie asked.

'Yes, now go,' said Woody. He used his pull string like a lasso and secured it around a bolt protruding from the landing gear.

Woody and Jessie swung down, landing beside Buzz on Bullseye's back.

'Yeee-haaa!' Woody shouted. He disconnected his pull string as the plane was picking up speed, escaping just in time.

'We did it!' Jessie shouted. 'That was definitely Woody's finest hour!'

'Nice ropin', cowboy,' said Buzz. He handed Woody his hat, which had fallen off earlier.

'Let's go home,' said Woody.

CHAPTER TWENTY-ONE

The Davis van pulled up at the house and stopped. Andy jumped out and ran towards the front door. He burst into his bedroom and jumped on to his chair, searching along his shelf for Woody. But all he could find were some dusty old books.

Disappointed, he turned and looked around the room. On his bed he saw 'Welcome Home, Andy', spelled out on Etch. Surrounding Etch were all his toys, plus Jessie and Bullseye. Overjoyed, Andy jumped down from the chair and picked up Woody, Jessie and Bullseye. 'Oh wow! Thanks, Mum!'

Andy was playing with his toys. 'Woody and the cowgirl fly across the Snake River Canyon . . . Oh no! They're attacked by a ferocious dinosaur. Rooaar!' said Andy, picking up Rex and mashing him into Bullseye.

'Help, help, somebody! A dinosaur's eatin' my horse!' Andy said, in Jessie's voice.

'Buzz Lightyear flies in to save the day,' Andy continued. 'Take that, dinosaur,' he said in Buzz's voice.

'Andy, breakfast is ready,' Mrs Davis called.

'OK, Mum. Be there in a second,' Andy shouted. Before he left, Andy wrote his name on the sole of Jessie's boot, and then he ran out.

As soon as he had left, Jessie grinned and showed her boot to Bullseye. 'Yeehaw!' she said. 'We're part of a family again, huh, Bullseye?'

'Ahem,' said Buzz, approaching Jessie. 'I'd just like to say that your hair . . . it's a lovely shade of . . . yarn . . . Uh, gotta go,' he spluttered, turning away.

Jessie lassoed Buzz with her pull string and pulled him closer. 'Well, ain't you the sweetest space toy I ever met!' she said.

Woody came up behind them. 'Buzz has a girlfriend. Buzz has a girlfriend,' he teased.

Buzz blushed.

Jessie put her hands on her hips. 'He

does? Who is she? Well, she's gonna have to get past me!'

Meanwhile, the three aliens were gazing at Mr Potato Head adoringly. 'You saved our lives,' they chanted. 'We are eternally grateful.'

'You saved their lives?' Mrs Potato Head asked. 'My hero! I'm so proud of you.' She gave him a kiss. 'And they're so adorable,' she said, glancing at the aliens. 'Let's adopt them.'

'Daddy!' said the aliens.

'Oh no!' said Mr Potato Head. He slapped his hand to his forehead and fell backwards. His parts came loose as he landed on his back.

Meanwhile, Hamm was playing the video game. 'Hey, Rex, can you give me a hand over here? I need your magic touch,' he said.

'I don't need to play. I've lived it,' Rex sighed.

Hamm turned off the game, and Al's Toy Barn commercial flashed on to the screen.

'Welcome to Al's Toy Barn,' said a sobbing TV Al. 'We've got the lowest prices in town. Everything for a buck, buck, buck!'

Hamm and Rex watched intently. 'Crime doesn't pay!' Hamm said to the TV.

Woody showed Bo his arm, which Andy had wrapped up with sellotape. 'Andy did a good job, huh? What do you think?'

'I like it,' said Bo. 'It makes you look tough.'

Wheezy waddled over, squeaking.

'Wheezy, you're fixed!' said Woody.

'Oh yeah. Mr Shark looked in the toy box and found me an extra squeaker,' he said.

'And how do you feel?' Woody asked.

'I feel swell . . . In fact, I think I feel a song coming on!'

Mr Microphone tossed Wheezy his mike. 'You've got a friend in me,' Wheezy sang.

Woody left the festivities and walked over to the far windowsill. Buzz joined him.

'You still worried?' Buzz asked.

'About Andy? No,' said Woody. 'It'll be fun while it lasts.'

'I'm proud of you, cowboy,' said Buzz, patting him on the back.

'Besides,' said Woody, 'when it all ends, I'll have old Buzz Lightyear to keep me company . . . for infinity and beyond!'

Buzz and Woody laughed, and joined their friends.